D0575029

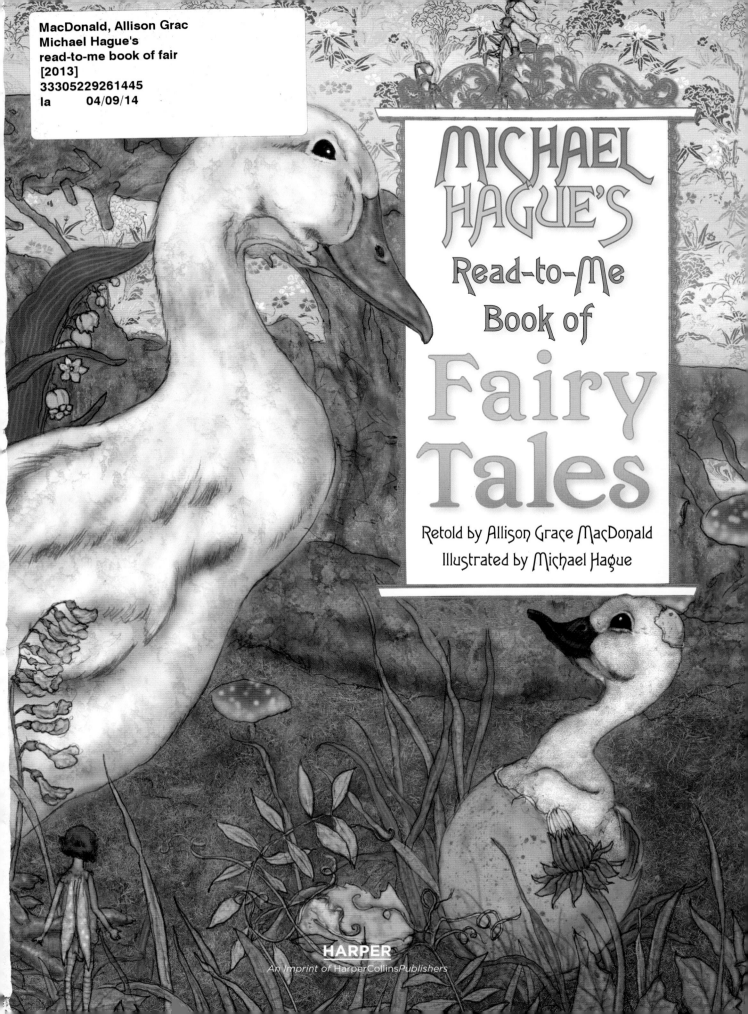

MacDonald, Allison Grac
Michael Hague's
read-to-me book of fair
[2013]
33305229261445
la   04/09/14

MICHAEL HAGUE'S
Read-to-Me
Book of
Fairy Tales

Retold by Allison Grace MacDonald

Illustrated by Michael Hague

HARPER

An Imprint of HarperCollinsPublishers

Dedicated to Bixby, Van, Aurora,
and Marigold.
With love from Cool Mike

Michael Hague's Read-to-Me Book of Fairy Tales
Copyright © 2013 by Michael Hague
All rights reserved.
Manufactured in China.
No part of this book may be used or reproduced in any manner
whatsoever without written permission except in the case of brief
quotations embodied in critical articles and reviews. For information
address HarperCollins Children's Books, a division of HarperCollins
Publishers, 10 East 53rd Street, New York, NY 10022.
www.harpercollinschildrens.com
Library of Congress Cataloging-in-Publication Data is available.
ISBN 978-0-688-14010-6
The artist used pencil, pen and ink, watercolor, and Adobe Photoshop
to create the digital illustrations for this book.
Typography by Jeanne L. Hogle
13 14 15 16 17 SCP 10 9 8 7 6 5 4 3 2 1
❖
First Edition

CONTENTS

Beauty and the Beast...1

Cinderella...9

Jack and the Beanstalk...21

The Little Mermaid...31

Little Red Riding Hood...39

The Nightingale...47

Rumpelstiltskin...55

The Seven Ravens...67

Sleeping Beauty...75

Snow White and the Seven Dwarfs...83

The Three Little Pigs...93

Thumbelina...101

The Twelve Dancing Princesses...109

The Ugly Duckling...117

BEAUTY
AND THE BEAST

There once was a man with three daughters who left home one day to seek his fortune. He asked his daughters what he could bring back for them. One asked for diamonds and jewels. One asked for dresses made from the finest silk. His youngest daughter, Beauty, asked for nothing but a single rose.

The man set out. After some time he came upon an old stone castle. In the garden was the most beautiful rosebush.

"Hello?" the man called as he opened the gate. No one answered. He knelt down to take a rose for his daughter, Beauty.

A shadow appeared and loomed over him.

"Who are you?" a deep voice bellowed.

Afraid, the man dropped the rose. "How dare you trespass on my property!" the creature yelled.

"I—I . . ." but in his fear, the man could barely speak. He looked up at the towering figure. The creature was large, with the fur of a bear and fangs and sharp claws.

"You are my prisoner now," the beast said as he grabbed the man by the collar.

"I was just picking a rose for my daughter," the man managed to say. "Please spare me!"

"A daughter?" The beast considered this. "I will let you go."

Before the man could give a sigh of relief and run away from the beast as fast as possible, the beast spoke again.

"I will spare you life—if you give me your daughter in your place."

Grateful to be free, the man rushed home and in tears told Beauty what had happened.

"It's all right, Father. I will go in your place," Beauty said.

She was always the most selfless of his daughters.

"But he is a great and terrible beast!"

Beauty ignored her father's protests. Satisfied that she was saving her father's life, she set off for the beast's castle.

The beast greeted Beauty warmly, and soon her fears dissipated. He gave Beauty anything she could ever want at the castle: dresses and fancy jewelry, servants to prepare her food and make her comfortable. She knew her sisters would be jealous.

Mostly, the beast left her alone, except every evening at nine o'clock, when he met her for dinner. They talked late into the night. And Beauty began to look forward to their conversations.

"Do you have everything you need, Beauty?"

"I do, Beast."

"Will you marry me, Beauty?"

"I can't, Beast."

Every night the beast asked Beauty to marry him, and every night she refused him.

Until one night when she asked, "Why do you keep asking me, Beast? I enjoy your company, but I can't be your wife."

Heartbroken, the beast asked Beauty to promise him that if she wouldn't marry him, then she would never leave him.

She had grown rather fond of him and wanted to make him happy.

"I will, Beast. But can I see my family one more time before I promise to stay here forever?"

The beast offered her a magic mirror that showed Beauty her family's home. Her sisters were married to wealthy merchants, and they looked happy. Her father, however, looked thin and pale, his face creased with worry.

"Oh, please, Beast. Let me go to my father. I must see him," Beauty begged.

The beast couldn't stand to see Beauty upset, so he let her go. He gave her a gold ring. When he put it on her finger, she would be transported back home. When she took it off, she would be transported back to the beast's castle.

Before she went to bed, Beauty put on the ring; and the next morning when she woke up, she was back in her father's house.

At the sight of her, her father's face lit up. She assured her father that the beast treated her well and that she was happy. Her father began to look less worried. As time passed, Beauty was so happy to be with her father and sisters that she started to forget about her beast.

Then one night she had a nightmare about her beast. She dreamed he was sick, with no one to care for him. The next day she said good-bye to her family. Beauty knew she had to return to the beast as she had promised. She took off the ring and was magically transported back to her bedroom in the castle.

Beauty called out for the beast but heard no response. Her voice echoed throughout the empty hallway.

From outside her bedroom window, Beauty saw something among the roses in the garden.

"Beast!" she cried, and ran outside. The beast was lying sick, barely able to move.

"You came back," he said, his words struggling to get out.

"Oh, my beast!" She cradled his head in her arms. "I do love you, and I will marry you!"

The beast closed his eyes, and in an instant he was transformed. Gone were the fur and fangs and sharp claws. In Beauty's arms, he turned into a handsome prince.

"I was cursed, Beauty. I was cursed to look ugly and frightening until someone would fall in love with me. I never thought you could love me."

"I do love you!" Beauty said. They were married and lived the rest of their days as king and queen of the castle.

CINDERELLA

Once upon a time, a beautiful girl lived with her evil stepmother and two evil stepsisters. The stepmother insisted that she wait on them, clean the house all day, and sleep in the soot of the fireplace. The stepsisters called her Cinderella because she was always covered in cinders. Cinderella followed their orders without complaint, but inside, she dreamed of leaving their house and falling in love.

"Stop daydreaming!" the evil stepmother scolded. "You can't sweep properly if you're not paying attention!"

Cinderella swept and scrubbed the floors until not even

a speck of dust remained.

"Make me breakfast!" demanded one stepsister.

Cinderella obediently cooked eggs, fried bacon, and served her stepsister.

"Fix these buttons on my dress!" the other, rather plump stepsister said.

Cinderella sewed the tiny stitches until her fingertips bled.

"Now go outside and tend to the chickens!" they both shouted.

So Cinderella went outside and fed the chickens and sang a sweet song about spring days to the field mice that poked their heads out of the grass. And this is how Cinderella's days slowly passed by.

One fine day a horseman galloped up the road and came to a stop before Cinderella.

"For the ladies of the house," he said with a slight bow, and handed Cinderella a large white envelope closed by the royal seal.

Before Cinderella could consider reading it herself, her stepmother and stepsisters appeared in the doorway. They politely waved to the retreating horseman, then raced to Cinderella as soon as he was out of sight.

"Who was that?"

"What did he want?"

"What did he give you?"

The evil stepmother snatched the envelope from Cinderella and tore it open.

She gasped.

"An invitation to a royal ball. **For all eligible ladies of the house.** My dears," she said to her daughters, "do you know what this means?"

"There's going to be a ball?" the plump stepsister asked.

"Well, yes, of course. But this means that the prince must be looking for a wife. Isn't this just wonderful! One of my daughters will be queen!"

"Ahem," Cinderella piped up. "It says *all eligible ladies*. Does that include me?"

"You? At a ball?" Her stepmother laughed, and the two stepsister joined in. "What would you possibly do at a ball? Sweep the floor? Don't be silly. Now, Cinderella, prepare our baths. I want my daughters to be irresistible to the prince."

Cinderella did as she was told. She drew water for their baths, she aired out their finest dresses, and she helped fix their hair. After they left for the ball, Cinderella went to her little bed near the fireplace and wept.

As her tears splashed into the soot at her feet, something wondrous happened. An old woman who glowed with magic appeared before her.

"Who are you?" Cinderella asked.

"I am your fairy godmother. Now, dry those tears. You have a ball to attend."

"But how can I?" said Cinderella. "I am just an ordinary girl. I have nothing to wear to a ball, and I have no way to get there."

With a snap of her fingers, the fairy godmother

transformed Cinderella's rags into an elegant gown of the finest silk. Her dirty brown shoes were replaced with silver slippers as delicate as glass. With a second snap, a magnificent coach lead by six white horses appeared outside.

Cinderella was astonished. Could all of this really be for her?

"You have only until the clock chimes twelve times, Cinderella," the fairy godmother warned. "The spell wears off at midnight."

Cinderella ran out through the doorway, not wanting to waste any more of the time she had left before the spell wore off.

✣ ✣ ✣

At the ball, the prince was on the dance floor waltzing with one of the stepsisters. Her sister waited jealously in the crowd. But the prince walked by her and caught another girl's eye. He excused himself to his partner and walked straight over to this beautiful and enchanting girl.

"May I have this dance?" the prince asked with a flourish.

Who was this girl who was important enough to steal the prince from her? wondered the stepsister. It was not anyone she had ever seen before.

It was Cinderella. Maybe it was her lovely gown or maybe it was the fairy godmother's magic, but not even her stepsisters or stepmother recognized her.

Cinderella curtsied and took the prince's hand. Her stepsister scowled and rejoined her mother and sister

in the audience. The prince spun Cinderella elegantly around the dance floor. Everyone watched and whispered and wondered who this mysterious girl could be. Cinderella kept her eyes only on the prince.

As one song ended and another began, the prince and Cinderella continued to dance. He looked at no one else, and he danced all of his dances that night with her.

✤ ✤ ✤

After hours had passed, the prince asked the girl to walk outside with him. He wanted to find out who she was and where she had been all this time since he had never met her before. Cinderella took his arm and smiled and walked with him.

"My lovely lady, tell me, what is your name?"

Before Cinderella could say anything, the clock chimed. It was midnight. Cinderella knew she had to leave before the twelfth chime or he would find out what she really was. With barely a good-bye, she ran out of the palace and toward her coach.

"My lady!" the prince called. Cinderella looked back one last time, tripping over the steps. The prince tried to rush after her to help, but she kept running, leaving

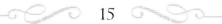

a single slipper behind. Cinderella leaped into the coach and rode out of the palace grounds as the twelfth chime sounded.

As she drove away, the prince picked up her slipper. He asked his footman if he had seen the beautiful girl running by. He said he saw no one but an ordinary girl in a drab dress. The prince vowed to find the mysterious girl with this lost shoe. When he found her, he would marry her.

The next day, the prince began his search. All the ladies in the kingdom wanted to try on the slipper, claiming that they were the prince's one truelove. But girl after girl failed the test.

✣ ✣ ✣

Then one day while Cinderella worked in the kitchen, a coach arrived at the door. It was the prince's coach! He was here to ask the ladies of the house to try on the slipper.

"It's mine!" the first stepsister said. She shoved her sister aside and grabbed the slipper from the prince. But her foot was too big, and try as she might, she couldn't cram her toes inside.

"No! It's mine!" the other stepsister insisted, taking the slipper from her. She tried to shove her foot inside, but her heel was too big for the delicate slipper.

The prince sighed. "Are there any more ladies in the house?" he asked. While the stepmother was encouraging her daughters to try again to squeeze their large feet into the slipper, Cinderella stepped out of the kitchen.

"Might I try, Stepmother?"

"You? I'm sorry, Your Majesty, this is only a servant. She does not know her place." The stepmother tried to shoo Cinderella out of sight.

Ignoring the stepmother, the prince met Cinderella's eyes. Could it be? Could this be his truelove? He knelt before her and held out the slipper.

It fit perfectly.

✣ ✣ ✣

Soon after, Cinderella and the prince married. Her stepmother and stepsisters bowed before her and begged her to forgive them.

"Do you promise to be good for the rest of your lives?" Cinderella asked.

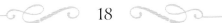

"We do," they said.

And they were forgiven.

Cinderella lived in the palace happy and in love for the rest of her days. Her dream had come true.

JACK AND THE BEANSTALK

ack and his mother lived on
a farm that had been facing recent hardship. A drought
had wiped out their crop for the summer and left them
with no food to eat or sell.

"Take our cow and see what you can fetch for it," his
mother said.

"But, Mother, without the cow we will have nothing
left," Jack said. But they were desperate. The cow was the
last chance for them to get any money.

As Jack led his cow to the market, a beggar passed by

them. Jack looked forlorn and desperate, and this gave the beggar an idea.

"I'm interested in buying her," the beggar said.

"How much money can you offer?" Jack asked, his face brightening. Perhaps this man could be their saving grace.

"I don't have money, but I do have these magic beans," the beggar said. "They will give you all the riches you can ever imagine."

Jack couldn't believe his luck! He knew his mother would be very proud at his bargaining skills. It was one thing to get money for the cow that they would quickly spend, but these beans would guarantee them money for life.

But when Jack's mother saw the beans, she was furious.

"You fool!" she cried. "Now we have nothing. Now we are going to starve to death." She grabbed the beans from Jack and threw them out the window.

Jack went to bed feeling guilty and with his stomach rumbling. Or was that rumbling coming from outside?

The next morning there was a huge beanstalk growing in their garden. It was thicker than any great tree and so tall that it reached higher than the clouds.

"I'm going up there to explore," Jack told his mother.

"No, Jack. It looks dangerous," she said.

Jack wanted to set things right. Against his mother's wishes, he scaled the beanstalk into the clouds. Higher and higher he climbed, until his house was just a speck below.

At the top of the beanstalk there was a house, more grand and prominent than anything Jack had ever seen before. Jack peeked through the window and spotted a loaf of bread on the table. Seeing no one nearby, he tiptoed inside and took a bite.

"Who are you?" a voice said from behind.

He spun around and came face-to-face with a very beautiful and very tall woman.

"I'm sorry, but I've traveled very far, and I just needed a small bite of bread," Jack said. He hoped that this woman might have pity on him.

Jack was in luck. The woman did want to help him. She sliced off a chunk of bread and gave him some cheese.

"Take this and hide," she said.

"Hide?"

"My husband is a terrible giant. He eats boys like you."

Just then the ground shook as the giant's footsteps came closer.

"Hurry! Into the oven."

Jack did as he was told. He jumped in the oven and watched through the vent in the back.

The front door burst open, and a giant ducked his head as he stepped inside.

"Fee fie foe fum," he bellowed. "I smell the blood of an Englishman!"

"Don't be silly," his wife said. "It's only the meat I'm cooking for dinner."

Jack watched as the giant sat at the table and feasted on

the biggest steak he'd ever seen. The giant then gobbled up a whole loaf of bread and had several glasses of wine. After all of the food was gone from the table, the giant looked restless.

"Wife! Bring me my goose," he said.

His wife gave him a lovely white goose. On the giant's command, the goose began laying eggs, but these were no ordinary eggs. Jack couldn't believe his eyes: these eggs were solid gold.

When the giant grew bored, he leaned back in his chair and closed his eyes. Soon the room was filled with the sound of snoring, loud enough to shake the whole house.

Jack quietly lifted himself out of the oven. He was going to make a run for the door, but those golden eggs tempted him. Instead, he climbed up the table and grabbed the goose.

Jack carefully and quietly made his way to the front door. Once he was outside, he ran as fast as possible toward the beanstalk. The goose began to squawk and flap her wings, but Jack was able to make it home safely.

Back in his little farmhouse, his mother looked doubtfully at the goose.

"Just wait," he said. Then he told the goose to lay her

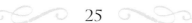

eggs, and when she did, they had a whole basketful of solid gold eggs. These eggs would fetch enough money to keep them comfortable and well fed for life.

Months passed. Jack was happy to have a full belly and not to have to worry about money anymore, but he couldn't stop thinking about the giant. What other magical things did he have that could make Jack rich?

Without asking his mother's permission, he set off one day up the beanstalk. Through the window, he saw the giant's wife alone in the kitchen.

"How dare you show your face here," she said. "My husband is distraught over losing that goose."

Before Jack could argue, he heard the familiar pounding of approaching footsteps.

"Quick, into the cupboard," she said.

"Fee fie foe fum," the giant bellowed. "I smell the blood of an Englishman!"

"Don't be silly," his wife said. "It's only the meat I'm cooking for dinner."

Once again the giant devoured the feast in front of him. After dinner he asked his wife to bring him his satchel of gold coins. He counted them and put them into stacks until he grew bored and fell asleep.

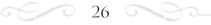

Before the wife could stop him, Jack came out of hiding and climbed up the table. He put the satchel of gold coins over his shoulder and ran.

His mother was furious with him for sneaking out, but then she saw the gold coins and was pleased. The coins were enough to buy them a bigger house and fine clothes to wear. They would never have to farm again.

This time three years passed before Jack had the urge to climb the beanstalk again. Golden eggs and gold coins—what else was the giant hiding?

Up the beanstalk he went. He walked cockier and a little more confidently now. He was no longer that desperate, hungry boy who had tried to take the giant's bread.

This time when he sneaked inside the giant's house, no one was home. He took his time looking in cabinets and closets, hoping to find the giant's treasures.

Then he heard the *thump, thump* of the giant's footsteps. Quickly, he jumped into a nearby washbasin and covered himself with soapy water. The giant couldn't smell him this time now that he was covered in soap. Jack watched as the giant's wife fixed him dinner, and he ate and ate until he couldn't fit any more food in his great big belly.

"Wife, bring me my harp," he said.

The giant's wife carried a golden harp to the table. The giant looked pleased. Much to Jack's surprise, instead of playing it, the giant commanded it to play. It sang the loveliest song Jack had ever heard. The song was so soothing that quickly the giant fell asleep, and his snores reverberated throughout the house.

Jack crawled out of the tub and shook himself dry. He climbed up the table and took the singing harp under his arm. Surely a magical harp like this would make him the richest man in his town.

When Jack reached the front door, the harp's song stopped. Afraid that this might wake up the giant, Jack began to run. The harp started to shout.

"Help!" it yelled. "This tiny man is stealing me!"

The giant woke up with a start, just in time to see Jack and the harp through the doorway. Jack ran with the harp and didn't look back. The rumble of the clouds was enough for him to know that the giant was close behind. He reached the beanstalk and began climbing down, with the harp crying in his ear and the giant getting closer.

When he reached the bottom, he called to his mother, "Quick! Get me an ax!"

Jack chopped at the beanstalk until it started to tip over.

"Push!" he said.

The beanstalk toppled over, with the giant on it. He crashed to his death in the fields nearby.

Jack's mother hugged him, happy that he was safe. Jack knew he shouldn't have risked his life like that. He was content and wealthy for the rest of his days, glad never to see a beanstalk again.

THE LITTLE MERMAID

Deep below the surface of the ocean, there lived a mer-king and mer-queen who had six daughters. When each of the young mermaids turned fifteen, their parents permitted them to swim to the surface and see the world.

The Little Mermaid was the youngest of the daughters, and each year she enviously waited for her turn to see the world above the surface. Finally, her fifteenth birthday arrived. The Little Mermaid anxiously swam to the surface and took her first breath of air. That night

was particularly stormy, and the Little Mermaid struggled to keep her head above the surface as the waves washed around her.

Just when she was ready to end her adventure and return to her home below the sea, she saw a large ship being tossed violently by the waves. The Little Mermaid swam closer, and there, among the wreckage, a handsome human lay unconscious across a broken piece of the ship.

There were no other humans in sight. The Little Mermaid knew that if she didn't help him, he would not survive. Swimming farther away than she ever had before, the Little Mermaid carried the handsome human to shore. As she looked into his eyes, she couldn't help but fall in love.

When the sun came up that morning, the human began to open his eyes. The Little Mermaid smiled at him, but before she could speak, she heard someone coming down the beach. Quickly, she jumped back in the ocean and hid underwater.

A beautiful maiden approached the human on the beach. "My dear prince, is that you?" She took his hand in hers.

A prince! The Little Mermaid had fallen in love with a prince!

"You . . . ," the prince sputtered. "You saved me!"

The princess smiled, didn't correct him, and helped him back to the palace.

The Little Mermaid knew she couldn't live underwater while her love was walking on land. She needed a way to get onshore and tell the prince that she was the one who saved him. She sought out the sea witch and begged her

to turn her into a human.

"On one condition, Little Mermaid," the sea witch said. "In exchange for a pair of legs, you'll have to give me your voice."

Surely the prince would recognize her right away, with or without her voice. He would know she was his truelove, the one who had rescued him from the wreckage.

"One more thing," the sea witch said. "The prince must choose you as his bride. If he doesn't, you will turn into seafoam."

The Little Mermaid agreed. The next thing she knew, she was thrust onto the beach, her fins replaced with clumsy legs and with no way to call for help.

A servant from the palace found her and helped her inside. When she was presented to the prince, he didn't remember her. Yet he was enthralled by her beauty. He volunteered to show the Little Mermaid around the city. The more time he spent with her, the more he realized that he loved the maiden whom he believed rescued him and not this quiet, clumsy girl.

The Little Mermaid continued to fall in love, but the prince wanted no one except the maiden. On their

wedding day, the Little Mermaid waited, grieving at the thought of becoming seafoam.

The sea witch approached her on the beach. The Little Mermaid wanted to beg for her fins back. She knew she had made a mistake. But of course, the Little Mermaid couldn't speak. All she could do was weep.

"My dear, my dear, stop your crying. I have just the thing to make everything better," the sea witch said. "I'll offer you another deal. If you use this dagger to kill your prince, I will let you return to the sea with your fins restored."

She left the dagger at the Little Mermaid's feet and disappeared into the water. The Little Mermaid wanted nothing more than to return home to the mer-king and mer-queen and her sisters. She hid the dagger and walked back to the palace.

That night when the prince was sound asleep, she sneaked into his bedroom and stood over him as he slept. She felt the weight of the dagger in her hands. But the prince looked so happy. Happy and peaceful. The Little Mermaid knew she couldn't go through with it.

She softly kissed the prince's cheek good-bye and fled the palace for the ocean to await her fate.

Instead of becoming sea foam, because of her kindness the sea witch transformed the Little Mermaid into a spirit of the air. She once swam in the sea as a mermaid and walked on the land on two legs, and now she could float forever among the clouds.

LITTLE RED RIDING HOOD

O nce upon a time, there was a young girl who lived with her mother. She was sweet and kind, and liked to believe in the good in everyone. Her grandmother, who loved her the most, sewed a red hood and jacket for her. The girl wore it all the time, and soon everyone called her Red Riding Hood.

One day when her grandmother had fallen ill, Red Riding Hood's mother sent her to go visit her grandmother and bring her food. She packed a basket filled with cake and wine.

"Be careful, Red Riding Hood. Don't stray from the path through the forest," her mother warned.

"I won't, Mother," Red Riding Hood promised.

"If you go into the woods, you could trip and fall and break the glass. Then your grandmother would have nothing."

"I will stay on the path, Mother," Red Riding Hood said.

Red Riding Hood set off and stayed on the path, walking quickly but steadily through the forest.

After some time she came upon a wolf, who stood alongside the path.

"Why, hello, little Red Riding Hood, where are you off to in such a hurry?" the wolf asked.

"To my grandmother's. She is sick," Red Riding Hood said, but she kept walking.

"And where does your grandmother live?" the wolf asked.

"Along this path. I'm halfway there. Her house is in the clearing below the oak trees."

"Why are you in such a rush? It's a beautiful day! I bet you haven't even noticed the lovely flowers growing alongside the path. Surely your grandmother would want some flowers to brighten her day?"

Red Riding Hood stopped. She looked to either side of the path. There were indeed flowers in every color she'd ever seen or imagined. Red Riding Hood knew Grandmother had been spending all day inside. She would appreciate some bright flowers to help her feel better.

Red Riding Hood decided to pick only a few flowers. Then if she just quickened her pace, she could arrive at Grandmother's on time.

✤ ✤ ✤

The wolf, of course, had other motives. He saw this lovely little girl and couldn't help but think about how delicious she would be to eat. But a meal of her grandmother too—now that would be the finest feast he had in ages.

While Red Riding Hood ambled through the wild flowers, the wolf raced ahead along the path. Sure enough, he spotted a house near the oak trees not much farther away.

He knocked gently three times.

"Is that you, little Red Riding Hood?" a small voice said from inside. "I am too weak to answer the door. Please unlatch it and come inside."

The wolf opened the door and walked into the grandmother's bedroom. Before she could manage a scream, the wolf swallowed her whole.

After one loud belch, the wolf quickly put on the grandmother's nightgown and nightcap and climbed under the covers.

✤ ✤ ✤

While Red Riding Hood searched for flowers, she kept seeing blooms more beautiful than what she already had a little bit ahead of her. Soon she was deep into the forest.

"Oh no," she thought. "I'm very late to visit Grandmother."

Red Riding Hood gently tucked the flowers into her basket and hurried back through the forest, finally finding the path.

When she arrived at her grandmother's house, she was surprised to see that the door was already ajar.

"Grandmother, it's me! It's little Red Riding Hood!"

"I'm in here," a raspy voice answered.

"I've brought you cake, and wine, and flowers, Grandmother," Red Riding Hood said. She stopped at the edge of her bed. Her grandmother had pulled her cap over her face and looked very strange.

"Why, Grandmother, what big ears you have!"

"The better to hear you with, my dear."

"Why, Grandmother, what big hands you have!"

"The better to grab you with, my dear."

"Why, Grandmother, what big teeth you have!"

"The better to eat you with, my dear."

The wolf leaped out of bed and lunged at Red Riding Hood, swallowing her whole.

✧ ✧ ✧

Soon after Red Riding Hood was eaten, a hunter passed by the window of Grandmother's house. He saw the silhouette of the wolf on the bed and thought it looked

very strange. He walked through the open doorway and saw the wolf sleeping on the grandmother's bed.

"Finally!" he said (the hunter had been tracking this mischievous wolf for years). "Here is my chance to get you once and for all!"

He was ready to take aim and shoot the wolf, but then he realized that it might not be too late to save the old woman. He took his knife and sliced open the sleeping wolf.

"Thank goodness!" Red Riding Hood cried as she gulped the fresh air. "It was very frightening in there."

The hunter helped free Red Riding Hood and her grandmother, then filled up the wolf's belly with large rocks. When the wolf woke up, he saw the hunter, child, and grandmother staring down at him. He stood up and tried to run at them, but the rocks inside him were so heavy that he collapsed on the floor, dead.

The hunter skinned the wolf and kept the pelt as his prize. The grandmother enjoyed her cake and wine and regained her strength. Little Red Riding Hood returned home safely and promised never to stray from the path again.

THE NIGHTINGALE

The emperor of China had everything he ever needed or wanted. He had the most expensive clothes to wear, the finest art to admire, and the most beautiful treasures to show off.

A soldier in his court returned from a trip and told everyone about the most beautiful song he had heard.

"When the nightingale sang, it took my breath away," the soldier said.

The emperor didn't believe him. His things were always the best, and this time would be no exception.

"Did it sing more magnificently than the loveliest

voice in my court?" The emperor ordered his most accomplished singer to sing her prettiest song.

"Yes, this bird's song was even more magnificent," the soldier said.

"Did it sing more beautifully than my prize bird?" The emperor ordered his servant to bring his best bird from his aviary to sing for the court.

"Yes, this bird's song was even more beautiful."

"What is the name of this magical bird?" the emperor asked.

"She is called the nightingale."

The emperor dismissed the man at once and demanded that he bring the nightingale to him. The soldier didn't know how to find the nightingale's home again. He asked everyone in the palace if they had heard of the bird. Only a maid who worked in the kitchen could tell him where the bird lived. They set out together.

The soldier, the kitchen maid, and members of the search party traveled into the woods. They tread carefully, not wanting to miss the sound of the nightingale.

"Listen! Over there," someone in the search party said. "Surely those notes belong to the nightingale."

"That is just the bleat of a young lamb," the kitchen maid said.

They kept walking.

"Yes! I hear it. That must be the sound of the bird near the stream," another said.

"That is just a chorus of frogs," the soldier said.

They kept walking.

Then they came upon the most beautiful song they had ever heard. The melody poured through the trees and danced in the air. It was light and moving and lovely.

They all knew that this was the nightingale.

"Dear nightingale, what can we give you that you might join us at the palace?" they asked.

The nightingale wanted nothing. She wanted to be free to sing and share her gift with as many people as possible.

✣ ✣ ✣

The nightingale came to the palace willingly and presented herself to the emporer. When the nightingale sang, he was delighted. Now he had every wonderful thing in China. He kept the nightingale in a cage and had her sing for every guest. He had her sing during dinner and in the afternoons. Her songs were different every time she sang, but they were all beautiful.

For the celebration of the emperor's birthday, he was presented with a bird made out of jewels. The jeweled bird looked like the nightingale. He could wind up the bird and it would play a song. The song was very beautiful, and the emperor thought it might be more beautiful than the nightingale's.

The emperor played the jeweled nightingale over and over again. Soon he lost interest in his real nightingale.

One night at dinner he asked that the real nightingale be brought to sing against the jeweled nightingale as a competition. After several rounds, the whole table was able to join in the familiar song of the jeweled nightingale. They clapped and cheered, and didn't ask the real nightingale to sing again.

No one noticed the real nightingale escaping from her cage and flying out the open window.

As time passed, the emperor grew older and became sick. He lay in bed, winding and rewinding his mechanical bird, until one day it couldn't sing anymore. The bird was broken.

The emperor sent for his real nightingale, whom he didn't know had disappeared years ago.

"We will find the finest jewelers and engineers and have them make you a new bird," his servants said.

But the emperor wanted the real, true nightingale back to sing for him.

The rumor spread through the kingdom that the emperor was dying. As the nightingale flew through the forest, she overheard people talking about their poor emperor. Without hesitation, the nightingale flew to the palace and perched on the emperor's windowsill.

The nightingale sang her best song yet. It was full of hope and love.

Death was so moved by this display of affection, he decided to spare the emperor. Quickly, the emperor recovered; and he reigned for many more years, with the nightingale in his court.

The nightingale became his personal emissary. She flew around the kingdom and relayed information about what she saw and heard to the emperor. She remained the emperor's most prized possession.

RUMPELSTILTSKIN

A poor miller sat in the pub with his neighbors one afternoon, and they took turns showing off by telling tall tales.

"I have the fastest horses—they win every race."

"My wife sings more beautifully than the finest birds in the sky."

Not wanting to be beat by his friends, the miller boasted, "My daughter can spin straw into gold."

They chuckled and gave the miller big pats on his shoulder.

One of the king's young and impressionable stablemen

was sitting at the next table, and he heard every word they spoke. A girl who can spin straw into gold! Surely bringing something as valuable as this to the king would get him into the inner circle of the court. The stableman rushed to the castle and told the king what he had heard.

Indeed, the king was interested, and the next morning they rode to the miller's shop.

The miller was quite shocked to see the king at his door.

"This man tells me that your daughter has a gift," the king said.

"M-m-my daughter has many gifts," the miller said, frightened that he might say the wrong thing.

"No need to be modest, commoner! I hear she can spin straw into gold."

The miller was taken aback. Before he could protest, the king sent his men to the back room. "Take his daughter and bring her to the castle. I will test this gift of hers."

All too quickly, the men had hold of the miller's daughter. She obediently followed them to their carriage waiting outside.

At the palace, the king showed the girl to a large room with no windows. It was stacked from floor to ceiling with straw.

"Spin this straw into gold," he commanded. "I will return in the morning to see that you are successful. If you fail, you will die." He shoved her inside, locked the door behind her, and stationed two armed guards outside.

"If she fails, you die too," the king said to the stableman. "For wasting my time."

The girl huddled in the corner and wept. What was her father thinking? She knew nothing of magic that could spin straw into gold. She knew this was her last night on Earth. Tomorrow the king would come, see all the straw as he left it, and execute her.

But then a small man appeared out of thin air.

"Who are you?" she asked between her sobs

"I am here to help you," the small man said. "I will turn all this straw into gold for you in exchange for the necklace you are wearing."

The girl gladly agreed. She sat back and watched as the little man took a handful of straw, ran it through the spinning wheel, and turned it into fine strands of gold. When all the straw had been spun, she handed over the necklace and the little man disappeared.

✤ ✤ ✤

The king returned the next morning with the stableman nervously hanging back behind him. The king was very pleased and ordered his servants to bring the gold down to the treasury. The girl was happy that her life had been spared, and she was looking forward to returning home.

But the king was greedy. He wanted more gold.

He filled an even bigger room with even more straw and shoved the girl inside, locking the door behind her.

"You will spin all this straw into gold by tomorrow morning!" he bellowed. "Or you will die."

"Your Highness—" the stableman began, hoping to be invited to court for finding this girl.

"You too," the king said. "If she fails, you will die too."

✤ ✤ ✤

Inside the room of straw, the girl paced back and forth, hoping for another miracle. Then the little man appeared.

"Oh, thank goodness!" she said. "Please help me."

The little man agreed, this time in exchange for the gold ring she wore.

He worked all through the night, and little by little the stacks of straw were transformed into gold. When it was all finished, he took her ring and disappeared.

The king returned the next morning and looked greedily at the room full of gold. This time he was prepared with carts to transport the gold to the treasury.

The king knew this girl was a true prize. Instead of letting her go, he escorted her to an even larger room full of straw.

"If you succeed in transforming all of this straw into gold, I will make you my wife," the king said. He shoved her inside and locked the door behind her.

"And you will become my most trusted adviser," he said to the stableman.

✤ ✤ ✤

The girl paced back and forth in the room, her heart racing with worry. Where was the little man to help her?

Just as she was about to give up hope, he appeared.

"Oh! Please help me," she begged. "I have nothing to

give you; but please, I need your help."

With hardly a hesitation, the little man knew what to ask for. "You must promise me your firstborn child," he said.

The girl was desperate. "Yes, yes," she said. "Whatever you want."

The little man went to work and finished spinning all of the straw just before dawn broke. He left empty-handed, promising to return when her first child was born.

The king unlocked the door that morning and was very pleased. The girl had spun all the straw he had and turned it into gold.

"And now I make you my wife." They were wedded that same day.

✣ ✣ ✣

A year passed, and the girl, now the queen, gave birth to a beautiful baby boy. The little man appeared at her bedside and demanded she give him the child.

"He is my son and the heir to the crown. I will not give him to you," she said to the little man.

"I'm a reasonable person," the little man said. "I'll make you a deal. If you can guess my name, you can keep your

child. I will return every night for three nights and give you as many guesses as you'd like. But if after three days you still haven't figured out my name, then the boy is mine."

✜ ✜ ✜

The next night as promised, the little man returned. He stood next to the queen's bed with his arms crossed, shaking his head at each name she spoke.

"It is Caspar? Petruche? Isore?"

"No. No. No."

The queen tried to recall every name both ordinary and strange that she'd ever heard, but none of them was right. When the little man had left for the night, she ordered a messenger to travel far beyond the mountains and report back any names he could find. She asked her servants to go into the kingdom, knock on everyone's door, and bring back any unusual names to her.

The second night when the little man had returned, the queen was ready with all the names her servants had brought from throughout the kingdom.

"Is it Albin?"

"No."

"Merigot?"

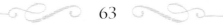

"No."

"Huroin?"

"No."

The little man left that night with a smile on his face. The queen was growing worried.

✛ ✛ ✛

The next afternoon the messenger returned. He said that far beyond the mountains, he came across a small cottage with a fire burning outside. He hid under the cover of the trees and listened to the man singing:

How silly of her to play my game.

Rumpelstiltskin is my name!

✛ ✛ ✛

That night the queen waited for the little man to appear. She held her son close, relieved that soon she could live in peace.

"All right, Your Majesty. This is your last night to guess."

"Hmm, let's see," she began. "Is it Saillot?"

"No."

"Bertrand?"

"No."

"Oh dear, what could it be. Maybe . . . RUMPELSTILTSKIN?"

"Who told you!" the little man yelled, and stomped his feet. In an instant he disappeared.

The queen never saw Rumpelstiltskin again; and her son grew up healthy and happy, and became king.

THE SEVEN RAVENS

man and woman had seven wonderful sons, but they wished and prayed for a daughter. Finally, the woman gave birth to a daughter; but she was small and sickly, and the parents worried about her. They sent their sons to the well to retrieve water for her baptism.

All of the sons wanted to help. They each wanted to be the one to save their sister with water from the well. They fought over the bucket, grabbing it forcefully from one another, until it accidentally fell down into the well. The seven brothers didn't know what to do.

Meanwhile, their parents waited impatiently for them to return.

"Where are those foolish boys!" their father said.

"Try to be calm," their mother said, rocking the baby girl gently.

"I curse those seven sons of ours. I hope they never return!"

With their father's angry words, the seven sons turned into seven ravens. They flew together back to the house and circled outside before flying up into the sky.

Their father hadn't meant to do such harm! He was just angry about their foolishness.

Soon after, the girl recovered. She grew up healthy and happy, and the parents devoted their attention to her.

✣ ✣ ✣

When the daughter was old enough to go to town on her own, she heard the townspeople whispering about her.

"Look," they said, "that is the girl with the seven brothers who disappeared."

"I hear her parents killed them."

"I hear they were turned into birds as dark as the night sky."

The girl rushed home and asked her parents if what the

people said was true. Did she have brothers? And what happened to them?

Her parents looked at each other and confessed. They had seven sons before she was born. They told her how selfish the brothers had been while getting water for her baptism and that it had been the heavens who'd cursed them and turned them into ravens.

The girl was determined to find her brothers and bring them home. Against her parents' wishes, she packed a loaf of bread, a jug of water, a stool to sit on in case she grew tired, and her mother's gold ring to remember her parents by. The next day she set off.

She walked all the way to the sun, but the sun was hot and threatened to eat her if she came too close. She then walked all the way to the moon, but the moon was cold and wicked. Finally, she walked to the stars. The stars were kind and helpful; they told her all about her missing brothers.

"They live in a secret cave at the base of the tallest mountain," the stars said.

"And how will I get into this cave?" the girl asked.

They handed her a chicken bone and told her to use it as a key.

The girl walked for miles and miles and climbed to the base of the tallest mountain. She reached into her bag for the chicken bone, but the bag was empty. Somehow the bone had slipped out on her long journey.

She had traveled all this way and now had no way inside! She looked at the keyhole. It was the perfect size for a bone. But would any bone work? Without hesitation, the girl chopped off one of her fingers and stuck the bone inside the keyhole.

The door opened.

The girl was greeted by a dwarf, who did not look happy to see her.

"How did you find this place? Shoo! Shoo!" he said.

"I am looking for my brothers," the girl said. She told him about her father's curse and about the trip she had taken to get there.

The dwarf invited her inside.

"The ravens are out right now, but they will return soon for supper," he said, showing her to his table. Lined up on the table were seven plates and seven cups. The girl was famished, as her loaf of bread had run out long ago. She took a bite from each of the seven plates and took a sip from each of the seven cups. At the last cup,

she dropped her mother's ring inside. Before the ravens returned, she hid in the shadows.

The seven ravens returned home and took their places at the table. They began eating but then paused.

"Has someone been eating from our plates and drinking from our cups?" they asked. Then the seventh brother saw something gold at the bottom of his cup. He instantly recognized it as his mother's ring.

The girl stepped out of the shadows and revealed herself.

"It's our sister!" the seventh brother exclaimed.

At the sight of her, the seven ravens turned back into seven men. They invited their sister to their meal, and the next day they set off to return home.

Their parents welcomed the seven brothers with open arms, happy to have their family back.

SLEEPING BEAUTY

A king and a queen prayed for many years to be blessed with a child, when finally their daughter was born. The kingdom rejoiced at the news of their new princess.

The king arranged for an elaborate christening to be held at the palace, and the most important people from near and far were invited. He asked the seven best-known fairies to bestow gifts upon the new princess.

But one very powerful fairy wasn't invited. The king and the queen hadn't heard from her in years, and they'd assumed that she was lost. When this disgruntled, forgotten fairy showed up to the christening uninvited, the king quickly set an extra place for her at the table. Unlike the other fairies, she had to eat from ordinary plates because there were only seven gold plates and those were already taken. The fairy grew angrier and angrier.

Then it was time for the fairies to announce their gifts to the princess. The sweet princess lay in her crib at the foot of her parents' thrones. One by one they lined up; and with a wave of their wands, they gave the princess beauty, grace, a beautiful singing voice, the ability to play any musical instrument, intelligence, and kindness.

The evil fairy then cut in line behind the sixth fairy to present her gift. With a flick of her wrist and a puff of smoke, she cast her spell:

"You, dear princess, who are beautiful and gifted, will have an unhappy fate. You will stick your finger upon the spindle of a spinning wheel . . . and die!"

Everyone gasped, and the fairy flew off before anyone could catch her.

"What are we going to do?" the king and queen asked.

"Excuse me?" It was the seventh fairy, the youngest of the group, who had not yet given her gift to the princess. "Maybe I can help. I cannot undo the fairy's spell, but I can do this."

With a flick of her wrist she said, "Dear princess, spindles might be your enemy, but they will not be your death. When you prick your finger, you will fall into a long sleep of one hundred years. Then your truelove will arrive to break the spell."

Immediately, the king ordered every spinning wheel in the kingdom destroyed, and the princess grew up protected and unaware of her fate.

✦ ✦ ✦

Not long after the princess turned fifteen, she was wandering on her own when she met an old woman spinning thread. The princess had never seen such a contraption! This old woman was new to the kingdom and didn't know about the king's decree banning all spinning wheels.

The princess was fascinated by the machine. She sat and watched the woman spin. Soon she became transfixed, as if she was under a spell.

"Would you like to try?" the woman asked.

The princess approached the spinning wheel and
pricked her finger on the spindle.

She collapsed, and the old woman called for help.
Representatives from the palace arrived and carried the
princess home. Her mother and father were devastated,
but grateful that she was breathing. They rested her in
the highest tower of the castle.

After a few days, the king and queen started to get
worried about what would happen in one hundred years
when their daughter woke up. She would be confused

and surrounded by strangers. They called upon the seven fairies and asked them to cast a spell over the entire castle. The fairies put everyone to sleep. No one would wake up until the princess's spell had been broken.

Everyone in the castle, from the cooks to the servants to every royal member of the household, froze in place. Their sleeping bodies slumped to the floor, where they would remain for one hundred years.

Over time the brush and brambles surrounding the castle grew higher and thicker, so any passerby wouldn't recognize it.

One hundred years passed, and many rumors about the castle and its people spread to nearby kingdoms.

One day a prince from a neighboring land was out hunting. His dog had run off in search of the next kill. Far away from the hunting party, the prince came upon the thicket surrounding the castle. He looked up and saw the tower high above.

When he returned to his group, he asked them whose castle it was. Everyone had different stories about diseases and curses, and said that the castle was abandoned. But when he returned home and mentioned it to his father, the king told him the tale of the sleeping princess. It was a story that had been told to him when he was a boy.

The prince knew that was the true story, and he was determined to save this helpless princess. He rode with his best men to the base of the castle. The brambles untangled before his eyes, revealing a wide path directly to the front door of the castle. He quickly rode toward the castle; but when he looked behind him, he was all alone. The path had revealed itself only to him.

The prince rode up to the gate, passing the bodies of townspeople and guards along the way. Were they all dead? He dismounted his horse and knelt before one of them. The man's cheeks were rosy, and he was still breathing. He was sleeping—just as in his father's story.

The prince entered the castle and walked up to the highest tower, where he saw the princess asleep, lying in an extravagant bed. She was more beautiful than he could have imagined; and without hesitation, the prince knelt down next to her and kissed her.

The princess opened her eyes and looked up at the man who'd saved her. Slowly, the spell lifted, and everyone in the castle woke up. The prince and the princess talked for hours (there were many questions to ask when one hundred years had passed). That night he

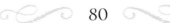

proposed to her, and she accepted.

The prince and the princess were soon married, and they ruled the kingdom and its people together, wisely and well.

SNOW WHITE AND THE SEVEN DWARFS

widowed king had a beautiful daughter named Snow White. When Snow White was still very young, the king remarried. Snow White's stepmother had a magic mirror she hung over her vanity. Every morning she asked her mirror, "Mirror, mirror, on the wall, who's the fairest of them all?" And the mirror would always respond, "You, my queen, are the fairest in all the land."

As Snow White grew up, she also grew more beautiful. She had skin the color of fresh snow and lips as red as

the loveliest rose. One morning when the queen asked the mirror as usual who was the fairest, the mirror said: "It's true, my queen, that you are fair, but young Snow White is the fairest of them all."

The queen seethed with jealousy. She could not stand to be outshone by her stepdaughter. The next day she hired a huntsman to take Snow White into the forest and kill her. The huntsman did as she asked, but he could not bear to kill the poor, innocent Snow White.

"Go, Snow White. Run away," he said to her. He told Snow White about the queen's plan and begged her to run away and never to return to the palace. Snow White

obeyed and disappeared into the forest. The huntsman killed a passing deer and took the meat to the queen to convince her that he had followed her orders. That night the queen feasted on what she thought was Snow White, satisfied that she had rid herself of her beautiful stepdaughter.

The next morning the queen looked into her magic mirror and, with a smug look on her face, asked, "Mirror, mirror, on the wall, who's the fairest of them all?" The mirror replied: "You are fair, my queen, but young Snow White is still the fairest of them all."

The queen was enraged. She had been deceived by the

huntsman and her stepdaughter. She knew that if she was to get rid of Snow White, she'd have to find her and kill her herself.

Meanwhile, when Snow White had left the huntsman, she'd wandered through the forest until she found a small cottage.

"Hello?" She peeked inside and saw seven small beds and no one at home. I'll just rest my head before anyone comes home, she thought.

Hours passed and Snow White lay in a deep sleep. As evening approached, she awoke to find seven dwarfs looking at her

"Oh dear!" she said. "I'm very sorry." She explained to them everything that had happened with the queen and the huntsman. The dwarfs felt sorry for beautiful Snow White and agreed to let her stay there if she kept house while they worked in the mines all day.

Snow White eagerly agreed. Every day she cleaned the house and cooked for them, and the seven dwarfs returned home to a clean house and a hot meal.

One day while the seven dwarfs were at work, a ragged peddler knocked on the cottage door.

"Excuse me, miss," the peddler said. "Would you like to

buy some silk lace?"

"What beautiful lace!" Snow White exclaimed, and she invited the old peddler inside. Snow White was such an innocent, trusting young woman that she didn't see the harm in inviting this poor old woman inside. But unbeknown to her, the peddler was in fact the queen in disguise! As soon as the queen was inside, she took the silk lace and tied her up. Snow White fell down as if she were dead.

When the dwarfs returned home, they found their Snow White on the floor, stiff and not breathing. "Quickly!" they cried. "Unlace her!" They untied the silk, and Snow White breathed again.

"You must not let strangers inside, Snow White!" the dwarfs told her. "Be careful, and don't open the door to strangers."

✤ ✤ ✤

Back at the castle, the queen approached her magic mirror. She had an evil smirk on her face when she asked, "Mirror, mirror on the wall, who's the fairest of them all?"

"My queen, you are fair, but Snow White is still the fairest of them all."

Once again the queen had failed to destroy her stepdaughter. She devised another plan.

The next day the queen again disguised herself as a peddler and knocked on the dwarfs' cottage door.

"Go away! I'm not allowed to open the door to anyone!" Snow White said.

"I am but an old woman trying to earn some money," the queen said. "I have beautiful combs to sell to beautiful girls."

Snow White couldn't stand keeping an old woman waiting outside. She let the peddler in and allowed her to put the comb in Snow White's hair. As soon as the evil queen did, Snow White fell down dead and the Queen left, laughing as she rode back to her castle.

The dwarfs returned to find Snow White dead on the floor of the cottage.

"Snow White! Snow White!" they cried. Quickly, they pulled the comb from her hair, and Snow White came back to life.

They warned her again about not letting strangers into their home. "The evil queen is trying to kill you," they said. Snow White promised she would obey this time.

Meanwhile, sure that she had already succeeded, the queen asked her mirror who the fairest was. The mirror once again said Snow White was the fairest.

Furious, the queen spent all night developing a poison apple. One side was white and safe to eat. The other was red and would instantly kill whoever took a bite.

✣ ✣ ✣

The following day the queen returned to Snow White's house disguised as an old peddler.

"I will not open the door!" Snow White insisted.

"I am just an old peddler, trying to sell some apples."

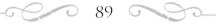

"No, I cannot let you in. Please go away," Snow White said.

"There is nothing to fear. I will take one bite from the apple, and you will see that it is harmless and delicious."

Curious, Snow White opened the door just a crack and watched the queen bite into the apple. The queen ate the white part and then handed the apple to Snow White, who took the shiny red apple in her hands and took a bite of the red side.

Before she could finish swallowing, Snow White dropped to the floor dead.

"Finally!" the queen cried. "Snow White is truly dead."

✤ ✤ ✤

The dwarfs returned home to find Snow White on the floor, pale and stiff. They searched her hair for poison combs and her arms for poison silk but found nothing. They couldn't do anything to help their dear Snow White.

The dwarfs put her in a glass coffin and carried her to a hill not far away. They laid her coffin among wildflowers and said their good-byes.

✤ ✤ ✤

The evil queen asked her mirror, "Mirror, mirror, on the wall, who's the fairest of them all."

"You are, my queen. You are the fairest in all the land," the mirror responded.

Weeks passed. Then one day a prince rode by on his way home to his kingdom. He saw a beautiful girl inside a coffin and fell in love with her skin as white as snow and lips as red as a rose. He asked the dwarfs if he might have this beautiful woman for his wife. The prince vowed to take care of her; and even though the dwarfs didn't want to part with her, they agreed to let him take her.

The prince's men came with their horses, ready to transport the coffin back to the palace. As they carried the coffin down the hill, the apple bite came dislodged from Snow White's throat. She awoke and sat up to see her dwarfs surrounding her and the prince standing over her. When her eyes met his, she fell in love.

Soon they married, and Snow White spent her days safe in her palace, with many visits to her dwarf friends.

THE THREE
LITTLE PIGS

One day three little pigs set out from home to seek their fortunes. Their mother gave each of them some food to eat and a little bit of money.

Not far down the road, they came upon a peddler with a cart full of straw.

"Perfect!" said the oldest pig. "We can build homes out of straw. And look how cheap! We'll have a lot of money left over." The other pigs weren't so sure. They let their oldest brother buy a bushel of straw from the peddler and continued on their way.

Next the two remaining brothers came upon a peddler selling sticks. They were more expensive than the straw. "But we'll still have money left over," said the middle pig. "We should make our house out of sticks."

The youngest pig wasn't so sure. He decided to say good-bye to his brother and continue on his own.

The afternoon passed, and the youngest pig walked alone along the path. Finally, he came upon a peddler with a wheelbarrow of bricks. When he asked how much the bricks cost, the pig found that he had just enough money to buy the whole bunch.

As the youngest brother was buying his bricks, the oldest brother was finishing building his simple straw house. He was able to relax all evening and go to bed early.

As the youngest brother laid his first row of bricks, the middle brother was finishing his house made of sticks. It was hard work, but he finished before sunset and had a good night's sleep.

The youngest pig stacked brick upon brick and carefully sealed each with mortar. He worked all night long and finally finished with the morning light.

Meanwhile, the oldest brother had a restful night's

sleep. Until suddenly, he was woken up by three hard bangs on his door.

"Little pig! Little pig! Let me in!" The oldest pig jumped out of bed and looked through the peephole in his door. It was a wolf!

"Not by the hair on my chinny-chin-chin!" he said.

"Then I'll huff, and I'll puff, and I'll blow your house down!"

The wolf huffed, puffed, and blew that straw house right over. But there was no little pig to be found.

That's because the oldest pig had run quickly as soon as the wolf started huffing and puffing. He ran down

the road as fast as he could until he found his brother's house made of sticks.

"Little brother! Help!" the oldest pig said. His younger brother opened the door.

"Quick! We need to hide."

Soon after they hid out of sight, there was a great big knock on the door.

"Little pigs! Little pigs! Let me in!" the wolf said.

"Not by the hair on our chinny-chin-chins," they said.

"Then I'll huff, and I'll puff, and I'll blow your house down!"

The wolf huffed, and puffed, and blew; but nothing happened. He tried again. He huffed, and puffed, and blew; and the house came down.

But there was just a pile of sticks and no little pigs.

That's because those little pigs had run away while the wolf was huffing and puffing. They ran as fast as their pig legs could carry them, all the way to their youngest brother's house.

"Little brother! Help!" they said.

Their little brother let them in.

"There's a wolf coming!" they said.

"Don't worry, big brothers; you'll be safe here."

Soon there was a loud knock at the door. The little pigs cowered out of sight.

"Little pigs! Little pigs! Let me in!" the wolf said, smacking his lips. This time they had nowhere to run.

"Not by the hairs on our chinny-chin-chins!" they said (the youngest a little more confidently than the other two).

"Then I'll huff, and I'll puff, and I'll blow your house down!"

So the wolf huffed, and he puffed, and he blew; but nothing happened. He tried again. He huffed, and he puffed, and he blew; but still nothing happened. The wolf was quite out of breath, and his stomach was grumbling.

He wanted those pigs!

"Okay, pigs. You win," the wolf said, trying to trick the pigs. He started to walk away but then tiptoed to the back of the brick house.

The youngest pig wasn't fooled. He watched that wolf through the window and figured out what he was up to.

"Quickly!" he said to his brothers. "Start a fire in the fireplace."

The older brothers did as they were told. They lit a stack of logs and got a strong fire going. Then the youngest brother filled a big pot with water and put it on the fire.

Meanwhile, the little pigs could hear the *tap, tap* of steps on the roof. The wolf was climbing as carefully as possible to the chimney. He reached the chimney, then leaped in face-first down to the boiling water waiting below.

Without hesitation, the youngest pig put the lid on the pot, trapping the wolf inside.

The three brothers had a feast of wolf stew that night, and the youngest brother promised that tomorrow, he'd show his older brothers how to build strong houses made of bricks.

THUMBELINA

There once was a lonely woman who longed for a child. She asked the witch who lived in the village (and was known to solve problems such as this) to give her the gift of a child. The witch said she would, and she handed the woman a tiny seed.

"But how—" the woman began.

"Trust me," the witch said. "Take this seed and plant it in the garden outside your house. All it requires is a little love."

The woman did as she was told. Quickly, the seed grew

into a green stalk that blossomed into a bud. The woman waited patiently, eager to see what would happen when the flower bloomed. When the pedals opened, there was a tiny baby girl nestled inside.

The woman picked up the girl and carefully held her in her hand. She was no bigger than her thumb and thus was named Thumbelina.

Time passed, and Thumbelina grew older; but she never got any bigger than her mother's thumb.

✥ ✥ ✥

One day as Thumbelina napped in a walnut shell, a toad passed by.

"My, my, that tiny girl would make a perfect wife for my son," he thought. The toad scooped up the sleeping girl, shell and all, and brought her to the river. Thumbelina woke up to find herself far from home in a strange place surrounded by toads.

"My dear girl, I would like you to meet your new husband," the tallest toad said, gesturing to the toad beside him.

"Husband? I'm not marrying you!" Thumbelina cried. She ran from her walnut shell bed to the edge of the water. The fish swimming nearby had heard her cries.

They offered her a lily pad on which to cross the river.

"We'll help you," they said. Thumbelina gratefully jumped on. A friendly butterfly pulled the lily pad down the stream until Thumbelina spotted a good place to stop.

Onshore, Thumbelina thanked the kind fish and butterfly, and set off on her own. That night she made herself a bed out of grass and drank dew from the leaves. There was a cornfield nearby with plenty of food to eat. Thumbelina realized that she was perfectly content living in the cornfield.

Then the weather grew colder. Usually when winter came, Thumbelina would live inside a warm house. She didn't know what to do when the corn stopped growing and her makeshift bed was covered with snow. She wandered deeper into the cornfield, and just as she was about to give up hope, she tripped on the edge of a hole and tumbled inside.

At first Thumbelina was frightened. But when she stood up, she saw that she was in a well-lit tunnel.

"And who might you be?" a friendly voice said. It was a mouse and his wife. Thumbelina introduced herself and asked for some shelter.

"Stay with us as long as you need to," the mouse wife said.

They offered her a bed in which to sleep and food to eat. In exchange, she helped them clean their home.

One afternoon the mice asked her to come visit their neighbor, the mole. They explained that the mole was very rich and powerful, and he lived underground all of the time.

Thumbelina knew it was important to the mice that she impress the mole. She sat with him and told him the story of her journey. He listened intently and was fascinated by her.

"Come," said the mole. "Let me show you my tunnels."

The mole led the mice and Thumbelina through the tunnels until they came upon a sparrow, lying motionless near the opening to the outside world.

"Stupid bird," the mole said. "Serves him right for entering my tunnel."

Thumbelina was shocked that the mole could be so cruel. That night she sneaked away from the mice's home to visit the bird. She knelt next to him and lay a quilt on his stiff body. But when she held him to give him a hug, she felt a heartbeat. He wasn't dead; he was just cold!

The sparrow opened his eyes and thanked Thumbelina for saving him.

The winter passed, and the mole grew more and more enamored of Thumbelina. She was always polite and never wanted to offend him. He took this to mean that she was in love with him. Thumbelina preferred to spend her time with the sparrow, who was still regaining his strength.

When the mole asked Thumbelina to marry him, she wept.

"I don't want to marry him," she told the mice.

"Don't be silly!" they said. "He's rich and rules all these tunnels. Why wouldn't you want to marry him?"

When she told the sparrow how she felt, he was much more sympathetic. "Fly away with me," he said. "I am healed now." He flapped his wings and hovered a few inches off the ground to show her.

But Thumbelina couldn't leave. "The mice have been so kind to me. They saved my life." That day she said farewell to her friend the sparrow and watched him fly into the spring sky.

Summer came, and her wedding day finally arrived. Reluctantly, Thumbelina put on her dress. She walked

along the tunnels, wanting one last peek at the sun
through the opening above.

"I suppose that once I am married to the mole, I won't
ever see the sky or sun again," she said.

As she climbed up the tunnel, a shadow approached
from overhead and swooped down next to her. It was
the sparrow!

"Hop on," he said.

Thumbelina knew she wasn't meant to live

underground and marry the mole. She jumped on the sparrow's back and gave a silent good-bye to her mice friends below.

The sparrow carried Thumbelina over the fields and into the biggest and brightest garden she had ever seen.

"I live in the tree over there," he said. "I will come and visit you when I can."

Thumbelina found a nice flower—just her size—that she could call home. How long had it been since she had last slept in a flower?

When she opened the petals, she was met with a surprise. A boy wearing a crown was inside, and he was just her size!

He introduced himself as the king of the tiny people. One by one, the flowers around her opened up and revealed a whole garden filled with tiny people.

The king offered Thumbelina a gift to welcome her to his kingdom: a pair of wings. Now Thumbelina was free to fly to the Sparrow's tree to visit whenever she liked. She had finally found a home.

THE TWELVE DANCING PRINCESSES

There once was a king and a queen with twelve daughters. The king was very protective of his daughters, so every night he locked them in the bedroom that all twelve shared. Every morning when he came to unlock the door, he found his daughters sound asleep. But there were fancy dresses strewn across the floor, and the shoes next to each bed were worn from dancing.

The king was furious. How could they possibly be sneaking out under his nose to spend all night dancing? He decided to issue a challenge to the kingdom: Any man who could discover where the princesses danced and how they got there could choose one of his daughters to marry. If he accepted his challenge, the brave man would have three nights to figure it out or he would face immediate death.

Eagerly, men of the kingdom lined up for the challenge. They wanted a chance to marry one of the beautiful princesses. How hard could it be to stand watch in their bedroom and see where they snuck off to?

But all of them suffered the same fate. They were locked in the room when nighttime fell and sat up watching the princesses sleep. Before they knew it, they were fast asleep themselves. When morning came, the princesses were still in their beds, but their shoes were worn from dancing. Three days would pass and then the king's guards would take them away to be executed.

✤ ✤ ✤

Meanwhile, a poor soldier was traveling alone through the kingdom. On one cold night he approached a house with a light on inside, knocked on a door, and begged for some food and a warm place to sleep.

The old woman who answered felt sorry for the soldier and welcomed him into her home. While he ate, the woman told him about the challenge that the king had issued.

"If only I could discover where the princesses dance, I could marry one and be rich," the soldier said.

"Maybe you can," she said. "I can help you."

The old woman told him to refuse wine at dinner and to pretend to fall asleep while he was keeping watch. She offered him a magic cloak that would conceal him while he followed the princesses.

✠ ✠ ✠

The next morning, after a good night's rest, the soldier rode to the castle and presented himself to the king. He would begin that night after the feast.

At dinner the princesses watched his wineglass carefully. But he was prepared. He put a sponge beneath his chin and let it soak up the wine as he pretended to drink.

When the princesses retired, he took his post in their bedroom, resting on a chair to keep watch. Soon they all fell asleep, and the soldier closed his eyes to pretend to do the same.

When all had fallen silent, the oldest daughter tiptoed out of bed to check on the soldier.

"Just like the others," she whispered. Then she gave the signal to her sisters to get ready. They all dressed in their finest gowns and put on their dancing shoes.

"I have a bad feeling about this," the youngest said. She checked on the soldier one more time, but he appeared to be sound asleep.

The oldest daughter knocked three times on her headboard, and the entire bed sank below the floor. One by one they filed into the darkness below.

Quickly, the soldier put on his invisible cloak and

followed behind them, careful not to make a sound.

Once they were belowground, the sisters tittered about the evening ahead, talking about the men they couldn't wait to see. The tunnel ended in a flight of stairs that opened onto a wide boulevard. The path was lined with golden trees that shone in the moonlight. The soldier plucked a leaf from the hanging branches so he might show it to the king.

"Did you hear that?" the youngest asked.

"It's just the trumpets, announcing the princes' arrival," the eldest said.

The boulevard ended at a lake, with a large castle in view. On the lake there were twelve boats, each with a prince waiting. The princesses each had fancied a prince, and one by one they got into the boats.

The soldier jumped into the last boat with the youngest princess.

"Why does the boat seem heavier tonight?" the prince asked.

"Maybe it is the weather," the girl suggested.

✣ ✣ ✣

Inside the castle a grand ball awaited, with music and dancing. Each princess danced with her prince. Everyone

danced song after song until the clock chimed three. At
three the music ended, and the princes escorted them
out of the castle and back into the boats. The princesses
looked tired but disappointed to end the night.

The soldier jumped into the boat with the eldest
princess, but she was too distracted to notice the extra
weight.

They waved good-bye to their princes and promised to
return the next night.

They crossed the boulevard lined with golden trees
and walked back through the tunnel. As they neared the
light at the other end, the soldier raced ahead of them

and jumped back into his chair, pretending to sleep once again.

"I don't think we have to worry about this one," the eldest daughter said when they returned to their room.

✣ ✣ ✣

When morning arrived, the soldier decided he didn't want to miss out on the fun the princesses were having by turning them in. He lied to the king and said that he'd slept the whole night. The next two nights, he once again followed the princesses. On the last night, as they danced, he took an empty goblet from the table, adding it to his collection of proof.

The morning after the third night the king arrived, ready to sentence the soldier to death. The soldier told the king everything: the tunnel below the headboard, the trees that shone like gold, the twelve princes, and the ball that awaited them. The princesses realized they had been caught, and they confessed that what he said was true.

The soldier chose the eldest daughter to marry, and they were married that same day, with all eleven princesses as attendants.

THE UGLY DUCKLING

A mother duck sat on her nest of eggs, waiting for them to hatch so she could show them the world.

One by one, the ducklings poked their beaks through the spotted shells and opened their eyes.

"There's my mom," one said.

"Look at this bright, beautiful world!" another said.

"Just wait, my ducklings. I'll bring you to the garden and show you how big and beautiful this world really is."

The mother duck and her new ducklings sat and

waited. There was still one more egg to hatch. This egg was larger than the rest, and dark brown.

"There's something wrong with that one," a duckling said.

"Yes, let's just leave it behind," said another.

"I bet it's a turkey egg."

Just then the brown egg cracked, and a beak pushed its way out. The duckling stuck his head out. He had long legs and brown fur. He looked at his duckling brothers and sisters, who were yellow and fuzzy.

But the mother duck knew these were all her ducklings. She had sat on the nest and never took her eyes off it.

"Come along, children," she said. She led them all to the garden pond. They followed her and dived right into the water, paddling in a line behind her.

Well, that settles it, she thought. A turkey wouldn't be able to swim. He must be my child, just a little different looking.

The mother duck taught her ducklings to swim and quack. The ugly duckling tried to quack, but his sound came out wrong.

"Who is that, and what is he doing here?" a passing duck asked the mother duck.

"He just stayed in the egg too long!" the mother duck said. "He wasn't properly formed."

Every morning the mother duck brought her ducklings to the pond to practice swimming, diving, and quacking. Every morning the ugly duckling was made fun of by his brothers and sisters and all of the other duck neighbors. They called him names and pecked at his wings.

One night when everyone else curled up to sleep, the ugly duckling sneaked away. He didn't want to belong to a family who was so mean to him.

✤ ✤ ✤

After wandering throughout the whole night, he came upon a group of wild ducks. He jumped into their pond and tried to blend in.

"Excuse me?" the ugly duckling said as politely as possible.

"What are you?" a nearby duck said. This duck was much bigger than the ugly duckling and had already started growing in feathers.

"I'm a duckling, just like you."

"You sure are ugly!" the littlest one said, and everyone laughed.

"Look around you," the father duck said. "You don't

belong in this family." Then they all turned their backs on him.

✣ ✣ ✣

The ugly duckling left the wild ducks in the pond and kept walking. Next he came upon a group of geese. The goslings were gray like he was.

"You're pretty ugly," a gosling said to him. The ugly duckling thought these geese were going to be just as mean as the other ducks, but then the father goose spoke up.

"Stay, new friend," he said. "You are welcome to join our family."

The ugly duckling was pleased. He didn't mind looking different from everyone else as long as they didn't tease him.

A few days passed, and the ugly duckling was getting used to living with the geese. Until one morning when a spotted dog came running through the reeds and started barking at him. The geese spread their wings and flew away as quickly as possible. But a hunter was waiting nearby and shot at them.

The dog came to where the ugly duckling was sitting and passed right by. For once the ugly duckling was glad

he was funny looking. At least the hunter didn't want anything to do with him.

In the melee of the hunter's attack, the ugly duckling hid in the reeds, then ran away unnoticed.

✣ ✣ ✣

By now the ugly duckling had grown some feathers, and he could fly a few feet off the ground. He flew a few miles from the geese and got caught in a storm. He took shelter under the cover of a cottage.

An old woman with squinting eyes saw the duckling through her window. She stuck her head out the doorway to get a better look.

"Is that a duck?" she said.

The ugly duckling was glad to be called a duck without any mention of him looking different.

The old woman welcomed him inside. She hoped that the duck would give her eggs to eat.

The ugly duckling spent all of autumn inside the old woman's cottage. Every morning she would come to his spot in the corner and ask, "Any eggs yet?" There never were any eggs.

When the first snow fell, the old woman had had enough. She was tired of feeding a useless duck.

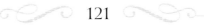

"There's something wrong with you, duck!" she said, then shooed him out the door.

The ugly duckling spent the winter huddled in an old log. He was very cold and very lonely.

✛ ✛ ✛

When spring came and the snow melted, he set off to find a pond in which to swim. The nearest pond was occupied by a family of swans. The ugly duckling was mesmerized by them. They were beautiful and elegant as they glided through the water.

In that moment, the ugly duckling wished that these regal birds would just kill him now. He'd rather be killed by them than pecked and ridiculed by ducks or have to keep living alone.

"Just kill me!" he shouted.

The swans approached him with their wings outstretched. He awaited death, but it didn't come.

"Come join us, friend," the swans said.

Join them? He took a few steps closer and then he caught his reflection in the water.

Staring back at him was an elegant white bird with a long, regal neck. A swan!

The ugly duckling—now a beautiful swan—ran toward

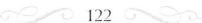

his new family. He was glad he had experienced the cruelty and disappointment of his life. It made him appreciate his happy new life that much more.

He swam behind his fellow swans to the other end of the pond, where children were throwing crumbs into the water.

"I want to give my crumbs to this one," a child said, pointing at the once-ugly duckling. "He's the most beautiful swan of all."